About the Author

I have been telling stories for eighteen years, since 1
this was got from my father who used to tell us stories when I was
young. I decided to write these stories down and this book developed.
I love the interaction of children and the look of excitement on their
faces as a story develops. I'd like to dedicate this book to my son Muiris
and my daughter Brianne who inspired all these stories.
Comments welcome to pippyanddippy@gmail.com

About the Illustrator

Maeve Keane is a writer/illustrator by night and a teacher by day. She
mostly likes drawing, reading and writing stuff. These are the first
of her illustrations to escape the cover of nightfall and make it into a
real-life-book.

Questions and comments can be emailed to Maeve
to mab.illustration@gmail.com

The Tea Party

Pippy and Dippy, the two curious mice that live behind the grandfather clock in the hall were always up to mischief. Dippy is the adventurous one while Pippy likes to tag along for fun.

One night Dippy decided to go up stairs, he climbed up along the banister all the way up to the top. Melissa had left her door open so he decided to peep his head in to see what was happening in side her room. As he went in he saw a beautiful figure standing on top of her dresser. Dippy had never seen anything so beautiful in all his life and he ran back down stairs to get Pippy.

"Pippy, Pippy" he said excitedly "come quickly I have something wonderful to show you".
The two mice ran quickly up the banister and back into Melissa's room.

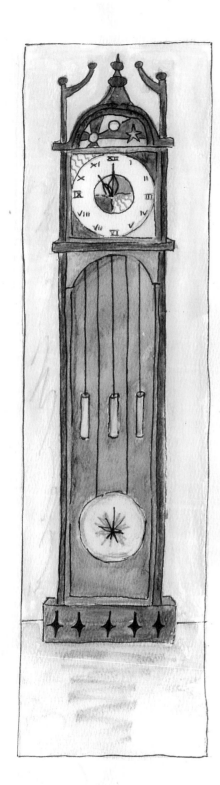

There she was, on top of the dresser, along side her was another figure who seemed to be drinking tea.

Pippy and Dippy climbed up on the dresser.

"Hello." They said, but there was no reply.

"Hello", Pippy said again. "Why aren't they answering, I wonder what the matter is?"

"I know!" said Dippy, "they are only dolls, and it looks like they are having a tea party."

"I'd love a party" said Pippy.

At that Dippy put the kettle on to make some tea and Pippy found a biscuit so they both sat down and had a lovely tea party with the two dolls.

All of a sudden they heard a loud snoring noise in the room.

"What is that?" They both said. "Quick hide."

Pippy and Dippy scampered off as fast as they could and hid behind the leg of a chair.

"That was a terrible noise I wonder what it was?" said Pippy terrified. "I don't know," said Dippy "it seamed to be coming from over near the bed." The two curious mice crept along by the wall, climbed up the blankets and onto the bed.

"Ho, golly gosh" said Pippy "look at the giant, and look at its lovely long hair, some of that would make lovely soft pillows for us, I wonder should we take some."

Dippy went over and pulled at her hair.
"Ouch" said Melissa, "what was that?"

She opened her eyes and saw Pippy and Dippy tangled in her long hair.
"What are you doing?" she asked.
"Your hair is so beautiful and soft we thought it would make nice pillows for us." They replied.

"You don't have to pull it out." She said, "The next time I go to the hairdressers I will bring some home for you."
"Oh, thank you very much." Dippy said.

Melissa asked Pippy and Dippy where they lived but before they could answer she fell fast asleep.

The two mice decided to explore further, so they scampered out of Melissa's room down the hall and into Alan's room. "Wow" said Dippy, "look at this!" "Cool!" said Pippy, "it looks like a racing car."

Pippy and Dippy jumped in and started it up. They drove like mad mice all around the room but as they took a turn they hit the locker knocking Alan's action figures onto the ground with a crash.

Alan woke with a jump. "What's that, who's there?" he said, "come out, come out."

With that Pippy and Dippy drove out from under the bed, out the door and down the hall, Alan jumped out of the bed and ran after them shouting,

"Come back with my car!"

But do you think he could catch them?

No way, they were too fast.

They turned at the end of the hall drove back towards Alan, and went under his legs so fast, he tumbled over with fright. They went back into his room again, parked the car and hid under the bed before Alan came back in.

Alan was puzzled as he looked around and scratched his head;

The car was where he had left it when he went to bed.

"I don't know what's going on," he said to himself maybe I'm dreaming. Alan crawled back into bed and as quick as a wink he was fast asleep.

The two mice had enough adventures for one night so they scampered back down the stairs, in behind the grandfather clock climbed into their nest and soon they too were fast asleep.

The next morning, at breakfast, Alan told Melissa that he had the strangest dream last night and told her all about it.
"That's funny" said Melissa, "I had a dream about two
mice as well."
Melissa and Alan started laughing.

Little did they know that it was not a dream, and Pippy and Dippy really did visit them and really do live behind the grandfather clock.

The Bottle

One night Pippy and Dippy went to explore the kitchen, as soon as they opened the door they got a beautiful aroma of something delicious. Pippy went to explore the floor while Dippy climbed up on to the counter.

Dippy thought the aroma was coming from the microwave oven so he climbed up on top of it, as he was looking around he saw a bottle next to the microwave he lent over to see if the aroma was coming from inside it, at that he lost his balance and PLOP!, he fell into the bottle.

Poor Dippy did not know what to do so he called out to Pippy to help him. "Help, help," he shouted.
Pippy heard a sound but could not make out what it was because the bottle muffled Dippy's voice. When Pippy looked up all he saw was an unusual figure inside the bottle. Pippy did not know what it was, but being the curious mouse that he was, decided to investigate.

When he got up to the bottle he discovered it was his pal, Dippy, "How did you get in there?" Pippy asked.
"Never mind that, just get me out of here," replied Dippy.

The two mice tried to think of a way to get Dippy out.
"I know." Said Pippy,
"If I drop something long and straight into the bottle you could climb out."

Dippy thought that was a great idea so Pippy set out to find something. All Pippy could find was a wooden spoon but it was too heavy for him to carry. Poor Dippy started to cry.

Pippy was so fed up he leaned up against the microwave oven door latch, the door swung open and WHACK! It knocked the bottle over, luckily it did not break, and Dippy was able to crawl out.

Once he was out the two mice scampered as fast as they could back up the hall and in behind the grandfather clock.

Just then daddy came out of his bedroom to see what was making all the noise.
"Is there someone there," he shouted,

He looked all around but of course
he could not see anything because
the mice were, by this time, tucked
up nice and tight in bed.

CHEESE

It was late one night, when Pippy and Dippy decided to venture out from behind the grandfather clock. As they were walking down the hall, what did they find?

A big piece of cheese!

Mummy was down in the kitchen a little earlier and made herself some crackers and cheese to eat in bed. On her way up to the bedroom she did not see the piece of cheese fall from the plate.

Pippy and Dippy could not believe their luck. The second Dippy saw it he ran to gobble it up as fast as he could but Pippy grabbed him by the tail to pull him back.

"Wait, wait," he said. "It might be a trap."
"Oh, oh" said Dippy, and stopped in his tracks.

The two mice looked very carefully at the cheese and walked around it making sure not to touch it. Then Dippy decided to touch it, so he crawled up really slowly… touched it… and ran away quickly.

Nothing happened so Pippy tip toed up and hit it with his tail... ran away fast, still nothing happened. "I don't think it is a trap," Pippy said after a while.

"I'm not so sure," said Dippy. "We had better be careful just in case."

He ran back to their nest where he got a lollipop stick, which he found a few days earlier. When he arrived back, he gave the cheese a poke and jumped back. Still nothing happened!

He gave it a harder poke but he hit it so hard the piece of cheese broke in half and Dippy fell over.

By the time he got up and looked around, there was Pippy sitting in the middle of the cheese, filling his mouth.

Dippy ran over as fast as he could and said "move over and make room for me."

Pippy and Dippy feasted on the lump of cheese and ate and ate and ate until their little tummies were BIG FAT tummies and there was still some cheese left over.

All of a sudden mummy's bedroom door opened, "I must have dropped that piece of cheese in the hall." She said.

Pippy and Dippy did not know what to do because they were too full to run and hide
"Oh," said Pippy "I can't move."
Just then Daddy called after Mum and said "it's too late I'll clean it up in the morning come back to bed."

Mummy turned around and went back into the room without getting a glimpse of Pippy and Dippy.

"Phew, that was close, come on, let's get back before somebody sees us," said Dippy.

At that, they pulled themselves up onto their feet. Needless to say, they weren't leaving the rest of the cheese behind them, so, Dippy got behind the lump of cheese that was left and started pushing it with his nose and Pippy got behind Dippy and started pushing him.

So they pushed and pushed and pushed until eventually they reached their nest, and got themselves and the lump of cheese in behind the Grandfather Clock.

The two mice fell into bed and they were so full they slept for two whole days.

A NEW FRIEND

One day when Pippy and Dippy woke up there was a strange scent in the air.

"What's that smell?" asked Dippy.

Pippy sniffed the air, "I don't know," he said, "let's go and investigate."

The two mice ventured down along the hall with their noses stuck in the air, smelling as they went.

"It's not food," said Dippy.

"No." said Pippy; "it's not food. I don't know what it is."

Then all of a sudden they heard a funny noise.

"WHAT WAS THAT?" asked Dippy.

"I, I, I D.D.DON'T KNOW." Replied Pippy "come on, let's find out."

As they went further down the hall they heard the noise again.

"Ooh" said Dippy "I'm going back to bed," and turned to run back up the hall. Pippy called after him, "Come back, come back, it's coming from in here."

Pippy and Dippy stuck their heads around the door to have a look to see what is making all the noise, they could not see anything different only a new basket in the corner.

What is it? They thought as the two curious mice made their way towards the basket. Something moved, and the two mice dived to hide.

Pippy looked over the top of the basket; "all I can see is a ball of fur." At that Dippy climbed into the basket. All of a sudden the ball of fur moved "Meow" it said. "Oh, oh, oh, qui, qui, quick, lets get out of here" Pippy said alarmed. "It's a Ca, Ca, Ca,"

"A what." Asked Dippy.

"A Ca, Ca, Ca," said Pippy again.

"What are you trying to say." Asked Dippy.

Just then a head popped out of the ball of fur, and Pippy fainted.

"Hello," said Dippy. "What's your name."

"Hello." The ball of fur replied. "My name is Fluffy, What's your name?"

"Oh, I'm sorry, my name is Dippy, and this is my pal Pippy. He must be very tired he seems to have fallen asleep," Dippy said. "Why are you making all that noise?"

"Because I am very lonely, this is my first time on my own," said Fluffy.

"Well you won't be lonely any more because we will be your friends and play with you," Dippy promised.

Pippy woke up in a panic, "It's a CAT, It's a CAT, quick Dippy run for your life, Cats eat mice" Shouted Pippy.

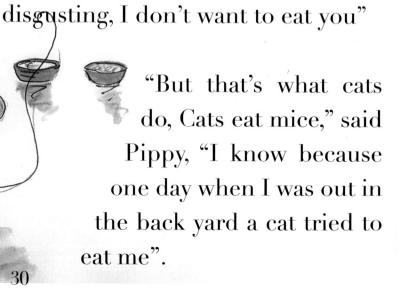

"Yuck,"said Fluffy, "Eat you, that's disgusting, I don't want to eat you"

"But that's what cats do, Cats eat mice," said Pippy, "I know because one day when I was out in the back yard a cat tried to eat me".

"aaagh, not this cat, all I eat is cat food and fish and drink milk," said Fluffy.

"Are you sure?" Pippy asked nervously.

"Come on,"said Dippy; "he's our friend."

"Would you like something to eat?" Fluffy asked.

"Yes please," said Dippy "I'm starving."

"You're always starving,"laughed Pippy.

"You're welcome to share my cat food," Fluffy said.

"Cat food! oh, no thanks," Dippy said.

"Well maybe you would like some milk?" Fluffy asked again.

"Yes please we like milk," Pippy accepted joyfully.

Pippy and Dippy drank the milk and Fluffy ate his cat food. The three became good friends and Fluffy was not lonely anymore.

THE JEWELLERY BOX

One night Pippy and Dippy were exploring in Mammy and Daddy's bedroom. Dippy was up on top of the dressing table, rootingaround, runningbetween the perfumes, Daddy's shaver and all sorts of things. He was having great fun.

Suddenly he saw a box in the corner.
He went over to it and he looked in.
There was a lovely glass top on it
and he saw lovely shiny things inside it.
"mmm, I wonder what they are" he said.

So with all his might he pushed open the lid on the box, up popped a ballerina, a beautiful song started to play and the ballerina began to dance. Well, Dippy got such a fright that he fell off of the top of the box.

"PIPPY, PIPPY, PIPPY QUICK,
Look at this," he said.
Pippy came running over.
"WOW, she is beautiful and look
at her dancing," he said. As the
music box played a lovely tune
the ballerina danced all around on a mirror.
The two mice stood and stared at the lovely
ballerina. They couldn't believe their eyes.

"Listen to the lovely music," Pippy said. "Let's take a closer look," said Dippy mischievously.

So he climbed back up on top of the box and looked in. All of a sudden, he tippled over and fell head first into the box this time.

"OUCH" he said.

"Are you OK, Dippy" shouted Pippy.

"I think so, but I'm all tangled up."

"What do you mean you're all tangled up."

"I don't know, I'm all tangled up," he said.

So Pippy took a look in over the top of the box and there was Dippy with all the jewellery wrapped around him. He got a ring stuck on his head, the chain wrapped around his feet and a cufflink tied onto his tail.

"Oh Dippy, how did you manage that?" he said.

"I don't know. Help, get me free," Dippy said.

So Pippy jumped into the box and untangled the cufflink from his tail first.

"What about my legs? What about my legs?" he said.

So then he went down and untangled the chain off one foot, twisted it around and wrapped it up then down and untangled it from the other foot, eventually after a lot of struggling, he untangled the chain from Dippys feet.

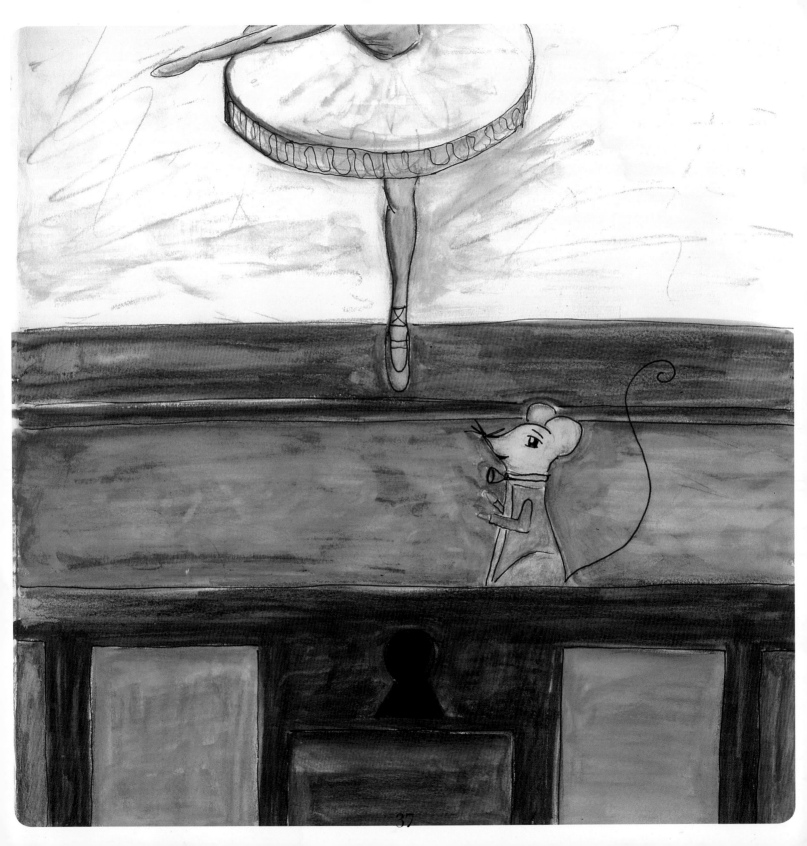

"What about this big thing stuck on my head?" he said.

"Alright so, I'll try and pull it from this end and you try to pull out your head".

So Pippy caught a hold of the ring and pulled and pulled and Dippy pushed away from him and wriggled and giggled and wriggled and jiggled. But the ring wouldn't come off over his ears.

"Oh no, what are we going to do now?" cried Dippy.
At that they heard a sound.
"Someone's coming, QUICK,"shouted Pippy.

Pippy and Dippy jumped out of the music box, climbed down and ran in under the bed to hide.
Just then, Mummy came into the bedroom.

"Alan, Melissa, were you two at my jewellery box?"

"No Mummy," they replied.

"Come up here. I think you were,"

"We didn't Mummy, honestly," they both answered.

Melissa and Alan came running in to the bedroom.

"Look, who opened that? Melissa I know that you like looking at that ballerina. Did you open this jewellery box?" she asked.

"I didn't Mummy, really I didn't," she cried.

"What about you Alan, you like trying on my watches. Did you open the jewellery box?"

"No, Mummy, I didn't. Honestly, I didn't," Alan replied.

"I wonder how it happened so?" Mummy was puzzled.

"I don't know. We didn't do it Mummy, truly, and we wouldn't tell you a lie," they said.

Mummy looked into her jewellery box and all the jewellery was higgeldy piggeldy all over the place.

"Oh my god, there's an awful mess. It looks like someone was playing football in my jewellery box," she said.

39

So she tidied it all up and put it all back but she noticed that something was missing.

"Ah, my ring. My ring is gone. Daddy, come quick, my ring is missing. did you take it? It's missing from my jewellery box," she said.

"No, I didn't see it anywhere. There must have been somebody in the house," Dad replied.

"I hope it wasn't the magpies from those trees," she feared, "I left the window open. I hope they didn't steal my ring".

"Ah no, they couldn't come in the window and go out again that fast without us seeing them".

"Oh no" said mummy "What are we going to do".
Pippy and Dippy heard all the commotion and were terrified that they will be found.

After a while they all went back down to the sitting room and Pippy and Dippy ran out of the bedroom, down the hall and in behind the grandfather clock.

"Oh no, what will we do'" they wondered.

So Pippy and Dippy sat down and thought and thought and thought and thought. Suddenly Dippy got an idea!

"Pippy, if you go and get some soap out of the bathroom and get a thimble full of water, we might be able to make suds and pop it off," he said.

"That's a great idea, Dippy," Pippy said.

So Pippy ran off into the bathroom, climbed up the sink and got some soap, filled a thimble fully of water and brought it back to the grandfather clock.

"Come on so," said Pippy.

Pippy put the water over Dippy's head and got the soap and washed and washed until there were suds all over Dippy's head.

"Yugh, the suds are in my mouth," he said, "Yaagh, it tastes horrible."
"Stop giving out," said Pippy, "Come on, let's get this ring off of your head.

Pippy and Dippy pulled and pushed and wriggled and twisted and pulled and pushed and wriggled and twisted some more. All of a sudden PLOP off popped the ring.
"Oh thank God," said Dippy, "It's off my head," when he looked over at Pippy.

Where do you think the ring landed? Right on top of Pippy's head!

"Oh no, said Pippy, look at this." Dippy pulled at it and luckily Pippy's head was a small bit smaller than Dippys and off popped the ring.
"Oh that was a close one" said Pippy "I didn't want to be eating suds as well".

At that, Dippy did a burp and a big bubble came out of his mouth.
"Quick, let's put this ring back fast," he said.

The two mice ran back, climbed up onto the dressing table, opened
up the box, the music started and up popped the ballerina dancing
again.

Pippy and Dippy stood and watched the beautiful ballerina.

All of a sudden, they heard a noise again. Mummy also heard the
ballerina.
"Quick Daddy, come, there's somebody up there now," she said.

The two mice dropped the ring and like a shot, were under the bed
again.

"Look," said Mummy "my ring is back again. I wonder how that happened"

"There must be fairies in this house," said Daddy.

"Mmm, I don't know," Mummy replied "there is something funny going on around here. But, at least I have my ring back".

So Mummy closed her jewellery box and locked it this time and off she went. At that, Pippy and Dippy went back behind the grandfather clock.

Dippys head was so clean he didn't wash it for a week.

Pippy and Dippy had many more exciting adventures but they will have to hold for another day.

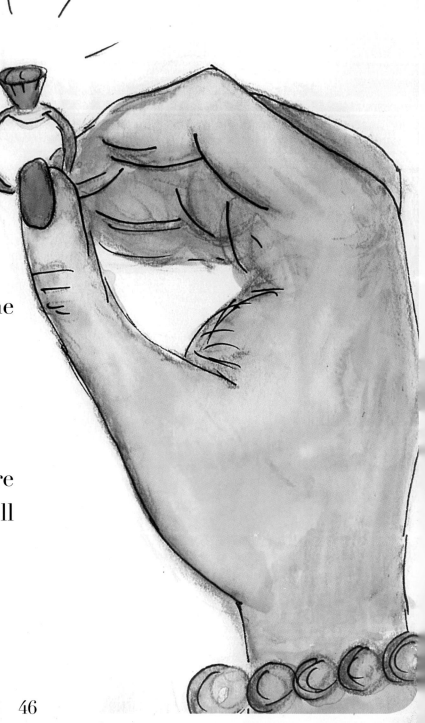